GO Diego GO!

NICK JR.

Diego's Egg Quest

by Cynthia Stierle
illustrated by Artful Doodlers

Simon Spotlight/Nick Jr.
New York   London   Toronto   Sydney

Based on the TV series *Go, Diego, Go!*™ as seen on Nick Jr.®

SIMON SPOTLIGHT
An imprint of Simon & Schuster Children's Publishing Division
1230 Avenue of the Americas, New York, New York 10020
© 2007 Viacom International Inc. All rights reserved. NICK JR., *Go, Diego, Go!*, and all related titles,
logos, and characters are trademarks of Viacom International Inc. All rights reserved, including the
right of reproduction in whole or in part in any form. SIMON SPOTLIGHT and colophon are
registered trademarks of Simon & Schuster, Inc.
Manufactured in the United States of America
10 9 8 7 6 5 4
ISBN-13: 978-1-4169-2751-8
ISBN-10: 1-4169-2751-4

¡Hola! Today is a special day, so my family is preparing a special meal. I'm bringing a basket of twenty chocolate eggs as a surprise for everyone. I hid it outside the Animal Rescue Center so it would be a big surprise. It's right over . . . hey! Where is my basket?

Oh, no! The Bobo Brothers are playing catch with my basket of eggs.
Help me stop them. Say "Freeze, Bobos!"

The eggs are wrapped in pastel-colored foil, so they may be hard to
see, but the Blue Morpho Butterfly will flutter around and help us look!

¡Fantástico! We found four eggs . . . with some help from Blue Morpho. ¡Gracias, Blue Morpho! So how many more do we have left to find? Sixteen! Come on! Let's look for them!

I'll use my Spotting Scope to see if there are some eggs near the river.

There's an egg on the other side of the river. But the river is so rocky here. How will we get to it?

Look, it's Baby Jaguar! He wants to help too. He can reach the egg because jaguars are great jumpers.

Let's help him. Find the shortest path so he can jump from rock to rock to reach the egg.

Thanks, Baby Jaguar! Let's keep looking. We have fifteen more eggs to find. Hey! The scarlet macaws are saying that some of my eggs landed in their nests. My Field Journal says that macaw eggs are white. Do you see any eggs that are not white in the macaw nests?

Thanks! Now I have my basket back, but where are the eggs?
Hmm. The Bobos must have dropped the eggs in the rainforest. We need to go on an egg hunt to get them back in time for my family's special meal!

Wow, look at all of these Blue Morpho Butterflies! *¡Hola*, Blue Morpho! Will you help us look for my special eggs?

Thanks for getting the chocolate eggs for me, Mommy Macaw. We found five more eggs!

Only ten more to go!

I wonder if there are more eggs in the treetops. This coati can help us! He's a great climber and has a good nose. If there are any chocolate eggs up there, he'll sniff them out.

Thanks, Coati! Now we've found almost all of the eggs. Let's see if any of my eggs are at Chinchilla Mountain.

Look! There are four more eggs up on that high ledge. It's too steep to climb the ledge, but Baby Chinchilla says she can jump up there and roll the eggs down to me. Chinchillas are great jumpers. Jump, Baby Chinchilla! *¡Salta! ¡Salta!*

We found all twenty of my chocolate eggs! I couldn't have done it without you. And I'm just in time for the special meal with *mi familia*. They're going to be so surprised! *¡Gracias, mis amigos!*